eleg

for angels, punks and raging queens

By
Bill Russell

Music by
Janet Hood

SAMUEL FRENCH, INC.
45 West 25th Street   NEW YORK 10010
7623 Sunset Boulevard HOLLYWOOD 90046
LONDON   TORONTO

IMPORTANT BILLING AND CREDIT REQUIREMENTS

All producers of ELEGIES FOR ANGELS, PUNKS AND RAGING QUEENS *must* give credit to the Author and Composer of the Play in all programs distributed in connection with performances of the Play and in all instances in which the title of the Play appears for purposes of advertising, publicizing, or otherwise exploiting the Play and/or a production. The name of the Author and Composer *must* also appear on a separate line, on which no other name appears, immediately following the title, and *must* appear in size of type not less than fifty percent the size of the title type. Billing *must* be substantially as follows:

(NAME OF PRODUCER)
PRESENTS

ELEGIES FOR ANGELS, PUNKS AND RAGING QUEENS

Book and Lyrics by
Bill Russell

Music by
Janet Hood

> *Because **Elegies for Angels, Punks and Raging Queens**
> evolved over several productions over a period of years,
> there is not an original cast which reflects the piece as it
> appears here. Characters were added, cut, changed and
> renamed. Included here are casts of the four productions
> which most contributed to the ultimate shape of the piece –
> two in New York and two in London.*

The first full staging of **Elegies for Angels, Punks and Raging Queens** was presented by T.W.E.E.D. *(Theater Works Emerging / Experimental Directions)* as part of its Sixth Annual New Works Festival, in association with Justin Ross. It opened on May 18, 1989 at the Ohio Theater in New York. The cast was as follows:

SINGER #1	Linda Langford
CHRISTOPHER	Kenny Morris
BILLY	Russell Garrett
TROY	Randl Ask
SEAN	Frank Jump
MITCH	Mark Fotopoulos
JOSH	Justin Ross
DOUG	André Morgan
SINGER #2	James Rocco
SINGER #3	Lewis Cason
TIM	Michael Kelly Boone
PACO	Sixto Ramos
FRANCIS	James Van Treuren
SALLY	Suzanne Rand
RAY	Bill Damaschke
DWIGHT	John Augustine
LAMAR	Stanley Wayne Mathis
JOE	Don Laventhall
MICHAEL	Laurent Giroux
ROSCOE	Jay Rogers
HELEN	Vera Johnson
PAUL	Lance McGinnis
NAT	George Cambus

```
CONSUELA . . . . . . . . . . . . . . . . . . . . . . . . . . . . . . . . Ajisha Terry
NORMAN . . . . . . . . . . . . . . . . . . . . . . . . . . . . . . . Phillip Officer
BERTHA . . . . . . . . . . . . . . . . . . . . . . . . . . . . . . Miriam Stovall
CHUCK . . . . . . . . . . . . . . . . . . . . . . . . . . . . . . Bradley Jones
HOWARD . . . . . . . . . . . . . . . . . . . . . . . . . John-Charles Kelly
OLIVER . . . . . . . . . . . . . . . . . . . . . . . . . . . . . Randell Fryman
ANDY . . . . . . . . . . . . . . . . . . . . . . . . . . . . . . . John Salvatore
NICK . . . . . . . . . . . . . . . . . . . . . . . . . . . . . . . . Tom McBride
GRANT . . . . . . . . . . . . . . . . . . . . . . . . . . . . . . Peter Bartlett
MILES . . . . . . . . . . . . . . . . . . . . . . . . . . . . . David van Leesten
```

A subsequent production at the RAPP Arts Center in New York opened on February 21, 1990 with the following cast changes and additions:

```
SINGER #2 . . . . . . . . . . . . . . . . . . . . . . . . . . . . . . . . David Ross
SINGER #3 . . . . . . . . . . . . . . . . . . . . . . Stanley Wayne Mathis
                              (until Lewis Cason returned)
CHRISTOPHER . . . . . . . . . . . . . . . . . . . . . . . . . . . Philip Bryce
TROY . . . . . . . . . . . . . . . . . . . . . . . . . . . . . . . . Terry Robison
MIKE . . . . . . . . . . . . . . . . . . . . . . . . . . . . . . . . Kenny Morris
JOSH . . . . . . . . . . . . . . . . . . . . . . . . . . . . . . . John Salvatore
DOUG . . . . . . . . . . . . . . . . . . . . . . . . . . . Edwin Louis Battle
TIM . . . . . . . . . . . . . . . . . . . . . . . . . . . . . . . . Michael Kane
                              (second half of run)
FRANCIS . . . . . . . . . . . . . . . . . . . . . . . . . . . Richard Conrad
TRACEY . . . . . . . . . . . . . . . . . . . . . . . . . . . . Lisa DeSimone
SEAN . . . . . . . . . . . . . . . . . . . . . . . . . . . . . . Randell Fryman
LAMAR . . . . . . . . . . . . . . . . . . . . . . . . . . Andre Montgomery
                              (first half of run)
CONSUELA . . . . . . . . . . . . . . . . . . . . . . . . . . . Natasha Hinds
NANCY . . . . . . . . . . . . . . . . . . . . . . . . . . . . . Carol A. Honda
NICK . . . . . . . . . . . . . . . . . . . . . . . . . . . . . . . John Schiappa
ANDY . . . . . . . . . . . . . . . . . . . . . . . . . . . . . Jorge Luis Abreu
```

The first London fringe production was presented by The King's Head Theatre and Giacomo Capizzano, opening November 10, 1992 with the following cast:

MELISSA *(Singer One)* .... Maria Ventura
CHRISTOPHER .... Jonathan Arun
BILLY .... Jonathan Brent
PATRICK .... George Heslin
MITCH .... Len Trusty
JOSH .... Aidan Dooley
DOUG *(Singer Two)* .... Omar Okai
BRIAN *(Singer Three)* .... Kevin Power
JUDITH *(Singer Four)* .... Sylvia Mason-James
TIM .... James Payten
TRACEY .... Amanda Mealing
DWIGHT .... James Lance
FRANCIS .... Patrick Duggan
RAY .... Mark Powley
PACO .... Carl Pizzie
SALLY .... Sharon Schaffer
ORVILLE .... Michael Bell
NICK .... Stuart Bennett
ROSCOE .... Lily Savage
                                            Regina Fong
HELEN .... Mary Chester
LAMAR .... Don Gilét
NANCY .... Polly Moore
KHADIJA .... Irma Endrojono
                                            Miquita Oliver
PAUL .... Brendan Coyle
NAT .... Simon Clark
RAFAELA .... Myriam Cyr
JOANNE .... Race Davies
TODD .... Joe Hutton
BERTHA .... Andrea Oliver
BUD .... William Vanderpuye
JOE .... Richard Pocock
GRANT .... Peter Birrel
MILES .... Ruairi Conaghan

The London West End production was presented by Giacomo Capizzano, Ltd. at the Criterion Theater, opening June 28, 1993 with the following cast:

Singers:

JUDITH	Kim Criswell
DOUG	Kwame Kwei-Armah
ANGELA	Miguel Brown
BRIAN	Simon Green

Actors:

CHRISTOPHER / PATRICK	James Dreyfus
BILLY / DWIGHT	Neil Roberts
MITCH / MILES	Ade Sapara
JOSH / JOE	Simon Fanshawe
	Alternate – *Derek Howard*
TRACEY / CHARLOTTE	Sarah Burghard
FRANCIS / GRANT	Graham Hoadly
LAMAR / WALTER	Don Gilét
RAY / BUD	Sean Mathias
TIM	Aiden Waters
SALLY / CLAUDIA	Trudie Styler
ORVILLE / NAT	Mac Andrews
NICK / PAUL	Stuart Bennett
ROSCOE	Regina Fong
HELEN / NANCY	Elizabeth Kelly
RAFAELA / JOANNE	Race Davies
KHADIJA	Gwyneth Jones
	Irma Endrojono
BERTHA	Nicola Blackman

Singer alternates	Maria Ventura
	David Arneil

Vocal Arrangements and Orchestrations by James Raitt.

ACKNOWLEDGMENTS

Many wonderful people have contributed to the evolution of *Elegies for Angels, Punks and Raging Queens* and it is impossible to acknowledge all of them. But a few must be mentioned:

Rita Mayer, whose editing of the poems was invaluable, Justin Ross, who nurtured the project in its early stages, Kevin Maloney and T.W.E.E.D. *(Theater Works Emerging / Experimental Directions)* who presented the first two New York runs with Justin, Bruce Bossard, who raised much of the funding for the early productions and, with Merry Morse, is a bedrock of the authors' lives, Ken Page, who premiered the piece in L.A., Mark Sendroff and Susan Steiger, who negotiated contracts over the years, James Raitt, who did the musical arrangements and orchestrations and produced the London cast c.d., Kevin Garrity, a constant and generous supporter and the extraordinary Giacomo Capizzano, who was determined to take *Elegies for Angels, Punks and Raging Queens* to London and ultimately the West End and did.

In addition, many fine performers, designers, stage crews, financial angels and friends have given their talents, skills, time, generosity and support to this project and we are most grateful.

And sadly, I think it important to note that many participants in the project's different incarnations are no longer with us due to AIDS, or are continuing to live with it daily. We especially want to extend our gratitude to them for reminding us why the piece was conceived and continues to be pertinent.

AUTHOR'S NOTE

Elegies for Angels, Punks and Raging Queens is intended to reflect the broad spectrum of people AIDS has both infected and affected. A correlative objective is to provide a vehicle which can involve a large part of the community in a theatrical response to the AIDS crisis.

Having directed *Elegies* ... several times in various circumstances, I have a few thoughts I'd like to share with other directors. The structure of the piece is not linear in the traditional sense but what is presented here has been worked out over many productions in front of many audiences. The rhythm, variety and flow of the running order have proven to be very effective and should not be altered.

Though it is possible for roles to be doubled (or more), I vastly prefer that the show be done with one actor in each role – making for a cast of 36! The piece has been presented with that size ensemble at the King's Head Theatre in London on a stage measuring 10 feet by 22 feet, so I'm convinced it can be done anywhere. An all-star benefit in L.A. used more than the four singers indicated here, which required less rehearsal time per performer and brought the company to 41. Though at first glance working with a cast of this size may seem daunting, the piece can be put together with minimal rehearsal time (excepting the director). I've often scheduled two half-hour rehearsals per actor (the singers require more) and then several group put-togethers and run-throughs. Because *Elegies* ... is often used as a fund or awareness-raising vehicle, participants (with the blessing of their respective unions) have frequently contributed their talents for little compensation.

Many of the characters are specific types, ages or ethnicities, but others could be played by wildly divergent types (some could even be either men or women). I've tried to give a sense of that in the following character descriptions. When casting this piece, I would encourage potential directors to reach beyond the talent pools with whom they normally work. If you have not worked with or don't know many older actors, children or members of different ethnic groups, here's a chance to broaden your contacts and make the production a true community experience.

I've found accumulation a most effective device for staging – starting with an empty stage, each actor remaining once having done the monologue. Since the songs are voiced in present tense and therefore reflect those still living with loss and AIDS' other ramifications, it seems fitting that the singers come and go.

A brisk pace is most beneficial. Eliminating lag time between monologues can help tremendously. *Elegies ...* is written in verse but that doesn't mean the actors should punch the rhymes. Better if they tell the stories as naturally as possible and let the verse take care of itself. Ad libbing seems not only unnecessary, but detrimental. Rhythm is everything in this piece and when extra syllables, creative comments and lengthy pauses are added, the results are less than satisfying (especially to the ear).

Speaking of the ear – a note about the music. This is not a typical musical-comedy score and the singers should be comfortable with pop styles. Janet and I lean toward hearing the songs performed on microphones, even in a small space. The style of the music lends itself to that, and the presentational nature of the piece does not make hand-held microphones seem out of place (though body mikes may make staging easier).

A word about the ending. I think it very important that the audience is briefly reminded of each character they've met. Giving each actor a moment to toss confetti in character and then to join in singing the final song allows for that and adds to the celebratory quality we'd like at the end.

My major advice, though, is to have fun with this, which is why I stress casting actors who can play comedy or find the humor in many of the monologues. Janet and I didn't intend for *Elegies ...* to be a dirge – rather a celebration of some very important lives. Oddly enough, something which came from such sadness has given us our most enjoyable experiences in the theater. I always tell the cast that it's fairly easy to make an audience cry with this subject matter – the challenge is to make them laugh. I also urge actors not to cry on stage – it undercuts that possibility for the audience.

We hope performers and audiences will come together to laugh, reflect on an incredible amount of loss and move to the beat.

bill russell
March, 1996

CHARACTER DESCRIPTIONS

I would stress the importance of casting actors from ethnic minorities whenever possible.

The SINGERS are wide open but a few considerations follow. All should be comfortable performing in pop styles.

JUDITH:
Soprano. BUD's sister, so those roles need to be coordinated.
DOUG:
Baritone. Has traditionally been black.
BRIAN:
Tenor. Should be believable as RAY's friend.
ANGELA:
Alto. CLAUDIA's secretary. Has often been black.

PATRICK:
A man in his 30s or 40s (old enough to have achieved success as a designer). Important that the actor can find the humor in the monologue.
BILLY:
Young (early 20s) a typical all-American mid-Western boy.
MITCH:
Any type, traditionally has been costumed in leather.
JOSH:
A clown and ring-leader of the group of friends (the first four characters plus DOUG).
TIM OR TINA:
Male or female teenager who can find the laughs in this. The younger and more energetic the better.
TRACEY:
Young, gorgeous, sexy and spoiled. She should find the laughs and stay away from pathos.
CHARLOTTE:
A young, tough drug-abuser.
FRANCIS:
A gentleman of a certain age. Outrageous.

RAY:

> *A regular guy, party animal, athletic. His friendship with BRIAN should be easily accepted.*

PACO:

> *An hispanic teenager, the younger the better.*

SALLY:

> *Many possibilities as long as she's not too old to have recently given birth.*

ORVILLE:

> *Middle-age, middle-class, "an ordinary Joe."*

NICK:

> *Drop-dead gorgeous, traditionally costumed in a towel, so a great body is a plus. The audience should be seduced by his charm and beauty.*

CHRISTOPHER OR CHRISTINE:

> *Any type male or female who can play comedy.*

DWIGHT:

> *A typical, young, Broadway-chorus-boy type, Southern accent can work.*

REBECCA:

> *Mid-Western, typical housewife.*

CLAUDIA:

> *A high-power corporate executive. A contrast to her secretary, ANGELA, is helpful. British accent can work.*

ROSCOE:

> *A big old drag queen.*

HELEN:

> *A typical grandmother.*

WALTER:

> *Old enough to attend a high school reunion, different somehow (ethnic? heavy? off-beat?) so we can see why he was something of an outcast.*

LAMAR:

> *A black, street-hangin', story-tellin' drug abuser. Essential that the actor find the humor here.*

RAFAELA:

> *A very young hispanic mother.*

NANCY:

> *Wide open as to age and type, but a no-nonsense kind of woman.*

KHADIJA:
Experience has proven that small, eight-year-old girls work best. Younger is heart-breaking but often includes projection problems. An ethnic minority is highly preferable and a boy (KWAME) is possible if all else fails.

PAUL:
A strong, leading man type with a great speaking voice. Old enough to have served in Vietnam (though he could have died from AIDS in the early 80s. He should be at least in his 30s).

NAT:
A fire and brimstone orator, traditionally costumed as a priest or minister. Should be at least 50 or preferably even older.

JOANNE:
Best comedienne available. Could be male (JOEL).

BERTHA:
Preferably black, middle-aged.

BUD:
Believable as JUDITH's brother.

JOE:
A comedian of any type or age, as long as he can get the laughs.

GRACE:
A professor type, strong dramatic actor. Often played by a man (GRANT), but now prefer a woman.

MILES:
Should be believable as DOUG's lover. Often cast with a black actor.

ELEGIES FOR ANGELS, PUNKS AND RAGING QUEENS

(JUDITH enters and sits or stands near the orchestra.)

"ANGELS, PUNKS AND RAGING QUEENS"

JUDITH:
WE PLAYED THIS DIVE IN THE VILLAGE
SOMEWHERE ON THE EDGE
DURING THE BREAKS I'D HANG OUTSIDE
HAVE A SMOKE SITTING ON A LEDGE
I'D WATCH THE PARADE AS IT PASSED BY
THE JUNKIES AND HOT-TO-TROT TEENS
AND IT FELT SO RIGHT
TO BE SHARING THE NIGHT
WITH ANGELS, PUNKS AND RAGING QUEENS

WE PLAYED THAT GIG FOR A LONG TIME
GOT TO KNOW SOME FOLKS
GAVE THEM SOME CHANGE OR TOOK THEIR CARDS
HEARD THEIR SCHEMES
LISTENED TO THEIR JOKES
SOMETIMES THEY WOULD STOP AND HEAR MY SONG
EN ROUTE TO THEIR FABULOUS SCENES
AND I STILL GET LAUGHS
FROM OLD PHOTOGRAPHS
WITH ANGELS, PUNKS AND RAGING QUEENS

WELL I LOVED THAT TIME IN THE VILLAGE
THOUGH I STILL DON'T KNOW WHAT IT MEANS
MATRONS AND WHORES
INTELLECTUAL BORES
ANGELS, PUNKS AND RAGING QUEENS

I PASS THAT PLACE LIKE A PHANTOM
EVERYTHING HAS CHANGED
THAT LOUSY DIVE IS A SLEEK BOUTIQUE
PRIORITIES REARRANGED
I LONG FOR THE MIX OF THE BAD OLD DAYS
THE BALLGOWNS AND TORN-UP JEANS
AND I SING THIS SONG
FOR THE SOULS WHO'VE GONE
SWEET ANGELS, PUNKS AND RAGING QUEENS

(Lights down on JUDITH, who stays in place. PATRICK enters observing JUDITH and indicating her when HE mentions his friends.)

   PATRICK: *(Part I)*
when i died
my friends
threw a fabulous party
exactly as i planned

with a chunk of my estate
in hand
they rented
my favorite restaurant
drank champagne and margaritas
laughed at memories
as tears and beers were spilt
unveiled my panel
for the quilt
then went dancing
and tossed my ashes
like confetti
on that ballroom floor
where we had played
and played before

oh we did know how to party
we heard the sound
of sirens in the city
calling us to join the dance
and met
in heady days of liberation
from our fears
a late-night celebration
of how right
it felt to say
i am here
and i am gay

yes
we sometimes went too far
too many drugs
too many men
but when that world
began to die
i marveled at the way
those movers of the stylish scenes
the stunning hunks
the disco queens
became the leaders of the fight
ever constant flames of light
in death's long and lonely night

the focus of my younger days
was largely split between
dad's body shop
and sewing on mom's old machine
me
the track and field star
working on my souped-up car
then whipping up fantastic frocks
oh not for me
or anyone
i always kept them under locks

but later on
those skills
of sewing and design
led to a modicum of fame
and many women wore my name

when i found out
my life would end from aids
i began to sew
the panel
which would show my name
upon this quilt

as i survey
all the thousands honored here
i wish that i
could throw them all a party
to celebrate
the lives they had

do not be sad
you who are the living
still have love to give
and troubled hearts to fill
with hope

we the dead
are free
of fear and strife
and of the mysteries of life

do not berate yourselves
for what you wish you'd said
before it was too late
honor us
with song and dance
and don't forget
to celebrate

(HE showers the audience with confetti and begins to dance as loud disco music blasts the theater. With a whoop, MITCH, JOSH and DOUG enter from all sides and dance with PATRICK in a tight group. From the opposite side of the stage, BILLY enters and surveys the dancing MEN. BILLY twirls, the disco music stops and the DANCERS freeze as HE addresses the audience.)

BILLY:
as soon as i could
i fled
the wretched town
in north dakota
its conventionalities
and cow-poke mentalities

i ran straight
to new york city
caught a cab
to christopher street
tucked my suitcase
at my feet
ordered something
a bit too sweet
and stayed 'til closing

yuuummm
glorious virility
overwhelming my eyes
like the disco sound
assaulting my ears
and the small town fears
floated right away
as i sat
day after day
watching the parade

life
life all around me
here in the village
no more dakota drudgery
instead
the neon-pulsed
manhattan-driven beat
of hunky boys
and men
complete with minds
set to compete
for the best this world
gives in one small place

these were the winners
of the race

so i got a job
and settled in
a studio
so long and thin
the sofa-bed
scraped the wall
when open
which was all the time
for who knew when
some stranger
dark
sublime
would stumble in
and leave me lying
with a grin
across my face
that even work
could not erase

but then
the plague descended
and my days of bliss
were ended
gradually at first
then growing
'til there seemed
no chance
of slowing
its advance

death
all around me
here in the village
the boys
the men
never to be seen again

and i among them
watching still
even here upon the hill
of the town
which i despised
ever glad
that i devised
some means of sweet escape

for though i was returned
by death
at least i set out after life
and found some pleasure
where i fled

MITCH:
i didn't do nothin'
that plenty of others
weren't doin' all along
so why was i
the one to die
by being hit
with this aids shit

god damn
it pissed me off
everything
from the doctors
to the cough
that wouldn't quit
gave me a pain
in my left tit

and just as a point
of reference
fuck the term
sexual preference
i didn't choose
to be this way
never wanted
to be gay
did not request
the "gift" of birth
and didn't want
my time on earth
to be cut short

forgive me
if i'm not a sport
about all this
but now that i
have kicked the bucket
all i have to say is
fuck it

(JOSH walks Downstage, crouches, pantomimes picking up something, then turns to the OTHERS.)

JOSH: Hey, here's a good one!

(DOUG, BILLY, MITCH and PATRICK crowd around, transfixed by what JOSH is showing them.)

JOSH: *(Continued)* Wait! Look at it wet!

(HE pantomimes putting the object in his mouth and then holds it up to ecstatic screams from the OTHERS.)

JOSH: *(Continued)*
tripping
on the beach
in provincetown[1]
the day was gray
the light diffused
whatever substance
we had used
made the hues
of tiny rocks
along the shore
glow like gems
in harry's store

and there we were
billy, patrick
mitch and doug and me
loony as five guys can be
jumping up in ecstasy
over each discovery
of another stone
whose brilliant colors
we would find alone
then share with all the others

---

[1] *Directors outside of the U.S. may substitute "mykonos".*

(JOSH finds one and runs back to the others.)

JOSH: *(Continued)* Look!

(Again the OTHERS crowd around.)

DOUG, BILLY, MITCH, PATRICK: *(In unison)*
Oooooooooooooooooooh! Aaaaaaaaaaaaahhhhhhhhhhhhhh!

JOSH:
someone had the revelation
that the unique configuration
of design
was more remarkable
when the tiny stones were wet
so we put them in our mouths
this sufficed more easily
than always crossing to the sea
oh we were loony as could be

"demosthenes"
i'd yell
"demosthenes
take those marbles
out of your mouth
and eat your dinner"

(The FOUR scream and laugh, hanging on each other. THEY form a huddle and freeze.)

JOSH: *(Continued)*
and everyone would scream
and carry on

how we'd laugh
at times like those
how sad those days
came to a close

first mitch got sick

(MITCH disengages from the GROUP and turns his back.)

    JOSH: *(Continued)*
we mourned him so
then the rest
began to go

(BILLY and PATRICK turn their backs.)

    JOSH: *(Continued)*
grief subsiding
not one bit
before another friend
was hit

when i succumbed
i fought the dark
which numbed my mind
by focusing
on when we shined
there on that beach

and my last request to doug
besides a final
healthy hug

(DOUG crosses, but it is JOSH who hugs him. Then DOUG crosses to one side.)

    JOSH: *(Continued)*
was that he take
my charred remains
and toss them
off that strip of shore
to blend with pebbles
evermore

i was ugly
as could get
and thought
i would look better
wet

(Music in as JOSH crosses Upstage and DOUG watches him go.)

"I'M HOLDING ON TO YOU"

DOUG:
OH THOSE DAYS WHEN LIFE WAS ONE BIG PARTY
FLOATING ON BALLOONS OF FANTASY
WHEN I'D FEEL SO HIGH
I COULD FLY RIGHT THROUGH THE BLUE
YOUR STANDARD REPLY
TO MY WELL-REHEARSED CUE
WAS "I'M HOLDING ON TO YOU"

(JUDITH enters.)

DOUG & JUDITH:
YES I'M HOLDING ON
CAN'T BELIEVE THAT YOU'RE GONE
I DON'T LONG TO PURSUE SOMEONE NEW
CAUSE I'M HOLDING ON TO YOU

(ANGELA enters.)

ANGELA:
STILL DON'T KNOW JUST WHEN THE PARTY ENDED
HAVEN'T STARTED LEARNING TO LET GO
I CAN'T SAY GOOD-BYE
AND CAN'T CRY FOR THOSE WE KNEW
I CAN'T EVEN TRY
TO DO MORE THAN REVIEW

(BRIAN enters and joins in.)

SINGERS:
SO I'M HOLDING ON TO YOU

YES I'M HOLDING ON
WON'T ADMIT TO WHAT'S GONE
AND DON'T LONG FOR NEW DREAMS TO PURSUE
CAUSE I'M HOLDING ON TO YOU

BRIAN:
FEELS LIKE WE'RE BALLOONING
THROUGH THE STORM CLOUDS
SOMEONE LET US LOOSE AND OFF WE FLEW
NO INSTRUCTIONS, NO CREW
NOT A CLUE WHAT TO DO
SO I'M HOLDING ON TO YOU

SINGERS:
YES I'M HOLDING ON
WON'T ADMIT TO WHAT'S GONE
AND DON'T LONG FOR NEW DREAMS TO PURSUE
CAUSE I'M HOLDING ON TO YOU

YES, I'M HOLDING
HOLDING ON
I'M HOLDING ON TO YOU
YES, I'M HOLDING
HOLDING ON
I'M HOLDING ON TO YOU

TIM:
i shouldn't be here
they got it wrong
no aids
not me
and that is why
i don't belong

i did get sick
and checked into the hospital
but quick

do i, doctor?
is it aids?
his studied silence
spoke in spades

so i took an easy exit
from my window
eight floors high
at least i died
on my first try

afterwards
the test came back
and showed
an overwhelming lack
of antibodies

i didn't have it
i was wrong
and now i'm where
i don't belong

this quilt is fine
for those who did
but not this kid

TRACEY:
i always got
what i went after
so when i heard
the music of his laughter
across that bar
where every self-appointed star
thought it wasn't cool to smile
i clicked my heels
across the tile
to his side
and said
"i have something to confide
i am completely over black apparel
it signifies a total lack
of individuality
i like your smile
and you're wearing red"

i knew he'd fall
into my bed

he did
one more slightly spoiled kid
who'd had it all
and wanted more
spinning my revolving door

except
i didn't send him back
to that world
all dressed in black
i kept him there
with me in bed
and bought him more clothes
colored red

then one fun night
of take-out
and videos
he bursts into tears

"i'm bi"
he chokes
"and i am sick"

and real quick
i jump in
"you're not sick
you're hot
no wonder guys want
what you've got"

"not this"
he cried
"not aids"

and when he died
he left me these
some crimson shirts
and his disease

i never thought
i'd end up dead
because i loved
a boy in red

CHARLOTTE:
god i loved getting high
any old drug
i was happy to try
and new medications
or combinations

telling a junkie
she could die
from sharing needles
is like telling the government
there's no more money

honey
it just don't register

so it was absolutely no surprise
when aids hit me
right between the eyes
that brought me down
so i searched the town
for a connection
to go the opposite direction

crack is cheap
but oooo it works
the drawback is
it comes with jerks attached
but having sex with twenty guys
can buy you several lovely highs

i ended on the street
"please, sir, spare some change
so i can eat"
and when a sympathetic passerby
dropped some money in my cup
i returned to shooting up

one day
this woman
looked right at me
said, "you don't look well"
my response,
"good enough to live in hell"

she took me to an office
filled with other chicks
putting in their do-good licks
by trying to get me help

oh i was sick
all sorts of female infections
which various inspections
showed were caused by aids
"sorry
those don't qualify
for government assistance"

even if i wanted
to get off drugs
which i certainly did not
"no room in rehab"
so if you're going
to buy the farm
what's one more needle
in your arm

that woman
and her liberated friends
did all they could
for those like me

they were cool
and they did try
but they weren't as good
as getting high

*(ALL on stage exuberantly break into the last bars of a piano bar
        standard. FRANCIS enters and sings louder and longer than
        anyone.)*

FRANCIS:
i'd lived enough
thank you very much
and was just as happy
it was over
though i wish the ending
wasn't quite so messy
and i'd died in something
a bit more dressy

still
i'm not sure
it was any worse
than living out
the age-old curse
of fading into
a tired queen
with a fallen ass
watching seasons
slowly pass
in some piano bar
wishing
i was young and firm
filling out
like a pachyderm

i was always first to scoff
at couples made
of two old men
i'd rather be a lonely hen
chasing after chicks

(HE approaches TIM who turns to him.)

who sometimes have the yearn
to learn
some antiquated tricks

(TIM laughs and turns away.)

   FRANCIS: *(Continued)*
the end
was not a pretty scene
though all-in-all
perhaps less mean
than years of me
growing old
and crotchety
always bitching
giving guff

oh, no, my dears
i'd lived enough

(RAY enters.)

   RAY:
my sister
went through men
faster than i did

   ALL ON STAGE: Ha!

   RAY:
well almost

some of hers were losers
some were boozers
some were cute
and one of them
was a real beaut

(BRIAN enters.)

RAY: *(Continued)*
that was brian
husband number three
or four
i don't remember anymore
he lasted longer
than the rest
but not forever
it was best

somehow
he became my friend
and we survived
the end
of their relationship

we shared the common bond
of loving sand and water
framed by a frond or two of palm
hot bright sun
and the balm
of island breezes
we dreamed of moving
to the tropics
of leaving
the aroma
there in soggy old tacoma

don't misconstrue
he was hetero
through and through
but we could do
most anything together
and have a real good time

*(RAY and BRIAN spontaneously break into pantomimed business.
    which illustrates their friendship – for instance, basketball,
    baseball or heavy-metal "air" guitar licks.)*

RAY: *(Continued)*
when i confessed
how messed up
i was inside
he took action
called in sick
said, "pick your island"
flew us to a beach
like that
where we just sat
and watched the tide
come in and out
discussed what life
was all about

and after we returned
he learned all sorts of ways
to help
how to change
my soaking sheets
without disturbing
all the tubes
how to give
the medications
how to fight
dull administrations
of hospitals and agencies
when to bark
and when to bite
and when to hold
my hand so tight
i'd see beyond
my fading sight

(BRIAN puts his hand on RAY's.)

of all the friends
i ever had
brian was the straightest
and certainly
the greatest

(Music in as BRIAN breaks from RAY, who lowers his head.)

"AND THE RAIN KEEPS FALLING DOWN"

BRIAN:
YES, MY FRIEND
IT'S RAINING AGAIN TODAY
I NEVER UNDERSTOOD
WHY YOU CHOSE TO STAY
IN A CLIMATE
THAT'S MOSTLY WET AND GRAY
WHEN WHAT YOU LOVED
WAS A SUN SO HOT
IT TURNED THE GREEN GRASS BROWN
AND THE RAIN KEEPS FALLING DOWN

I THOUGHT THE SKY
WOULD CRY ITSELF DRY
BY THIS TIME
THOUGHT THAT I
WOULD SEE THE SUN BY NOW
ONE MORE TEAR
MIGHT WASH AWAY
THIS GOD-FORSAKEN TOWN
BUT THE RAIN KEEPS FALLING DOWN

WHO AM I
A REGULAR KING OF GUY
I NEVER LET THE CLOUDS
CLUTTER UP MY SKY
LEARNED TO PARTY
BUT NEVER LEARNED TO CRY
AND EVEN NOW
MY TEARS WON'T MOVE
THEY'RE PAINTED ON A CLOWN
AND THE RAIN KEEPS FALLIN' DOWN

WISH THAT I COULD LET GO
LIKE THE STORM CLOUDS
BURST THROUGH THE DAM
LIKE A FLOOD BREAKING DOWN A WALL
HEAVEN SEEMS TO WEEP WITH FAR LESS REASON
BUT I CAN'T CRY AT ALL

*(Very slowly, EVERYONE Onstage crosses into a tunnel of light
and takes a seat.)*

    BRIAN: *(Continued)*
THOUGHT THE SKY
WOULD CRY ITSELF DRY
BY THIS TIME
THOUGHT THAT I
WOULD SEE THE SUN BY NOW
ONE MORE TEAR
MIGHT WASH AWAY
THIS GOD-FORSAKEN TOWN
BUT THE RAIN KEEPS FALLING DOWN

(RAY is the last to move to his spot. BRIAN takes one last look.)

    BRIAN: *(Continued)*
YES, THE RAIN KEEPS FALLING DOWN

(RAY sits on the last notes of music.)

(PACO enters.)

    PACO:
mamacita
mamacita soldano
mi madre of the heart
del corazon

my own mother
smashed a blessed porcelain virgin
on the floor
screamed, "get out"
and locked the door
no way to change her mind
i was gone
another sorrow left behind

mrs. soldano
chico's mom
tried to reason
with my mother
"whatever he has done
he is still your son"
but nothing could be said
to her i was already dead

so my new mamacita
let me stay
and came each day
to sit beside my bed
and pray

in my room
she placed a statue
of the holy mother
carved in burnished wood
whose silent smile
whispered that she understood my fear
and promised
that she would stay near

dear mamacita soldano
who treated me
like your own son
and never questioned
what i'd done
to end this way

mi madre wouldn't keep me
i never knew mi padre
but i found comfort
thanks to you
my dear adopted madre

*(SALLY enters wearing a coat. Seeing a prospective john, she
quickly opens it, revealing a very skimpy outfit, or none at all.
Not getting the reaction she was looking for, SHE closes the
coat in disgust.)*

SALLY:
figures
some guy
would give me this
they've always given me
so much

papa gave
the business
since i was ten
and if i cried
he tanned my hide
and gave gifts
which hurt
much worse
than his disgusting rod

then harry, dick and tom
gave me wedded bliss
a kiss
of violence
if their beer was hot
or dinner cold
or they were out of sorts
what sports

how many
gave me money
for a bit of head
i never was much good
at math
so i count tenderness instead

and then there were the dudes
who gave me
coke and hop and ludes
to dull the edge
help me relax
keep me chuggin'
down the tracks

with all the gifts
i got from men
i should have loved it when
i passed
the lethal present on

except
the man i gave it to
was my own boy
born with aids
a ticking bomb
which would destroy him

i guess it's best
he never knew
exactly what this world
can do
what kind of man
would he have been
with all of my
good will toward men

(As ORVILLE enters, SALLY flashes him. HE does not respond.
   SHE closes her coat with annoyance and crosses to her seat.)

ORVILLE:
i was an ordinary joe
took life
and even breakfast slow

i never scaled the heights
or even saw too many sights
i did my part
kept the book in order
and the cart
behind the horse
never wavered
from my course

except that time
when emily announced
she wanted a divorce
i walked out
with no emotion showing
the door
swinging on a broken hinge
and dived into
a most unlikely binge

me
awaking in a house
of ill-repute
where several things
did not compute

how i got there
what i'd done
if only my one lapse from grace
had at the very least
been fun

and in my bed
a little chick
with hair so red
it seemed
her sordid life
had bled
right through her empty head

this was not
the world i knew
numbers
columns
neat and true

i only visited
by chance
and left
that awful circumstance
as soon as i
could find my pants

my life was not like magic
no headlines screamed my fate
my death was not called tragic
by the fourth estate

living with the secret
i would sometimes overhear
other men make fun
of warnings they should fear
a plague of retribution
on those they'd not go near

somehow i could not tell them
what they didn't want to know
a virus isn't picky
about where it wants to grow
they never dreamed
it lived next door
in ordinary joe

*(NICK enters, wearing only a towel wrapped around his waist. HE
     is extremely handsome, muscular and charming and delivers
     the following as though discussing a pleasant day on the
     beach.)*

NICK:
i didn't give
a flying fuck
for anyone
no one ever gave
a fuck for me

i went straight
from the doctor's
where i got the news
that i would lose
this stinking curse called life
i went from that announcement
directly to the baths
and fucked every jerk i could

i'd finish
and he'd say
"daddy that was good"
i'd crack a grin
and slowly stick
the dagger in
"boy, it could be said
that i fucked you to death
'cause i have aids
now so do you
yeah, boy
now you have got it too"

i'd let that
sink in a bit
wait for tears
the little shit
then i'd quit
the lousy fuck's small room
and look for someone else
to doom

*(HE winks at someone in the audience and crosses to his seat.
Music in as DOUG and BRIAN enter. THEY exchange a look
upon seeing NICK in his towel.)*

"I DON'T DO THAT ... ANYMORE"

DOUG:
THERE WAS A TIME
I WAS KNOWN AS LOOSE
GANDERS WERE FINE
IF I WAS OUT OF GOOSE
CHICKENS FLYING
IN AND OUT THE DOOR
BUT I DON'T DO THAT
ANYMORE

BRIAN:
I USED TO DRINK
LIKE A DRIED UP WHALE
SWALLOW THE BRINE
'TIL I WAS ON MY TAIL
DIVE FOR GOLDFISH
ON THE BARROOM FLOOR
BUT I DON'T DO THAT
ANYMORE

BRIAN & DOUG:
NO, I DON'T DO THIS
AND I DON'T DO THAT
I DON'T LOSE MY HEAD
I DON'T TOSS MY HAT
I'VE TRIED IT ALL
AT LEAST ONCE BEFORE
BUT I DON'T DO THAT
ANYMORE

DOUG:
I MUST ADMIT
I'VE HAD SOME REGRETS

BRIAN:
AFTER THE RACE
YOU CAN'T CHANGE YOUR BETS

DOUG:
FEELING GUILTY
IS A TERRIBLE BORE

BRIAN:
SO I DON'T DO THAT
ANYMORE

DOUG & BRIAN:
NO, I DON'T DO THIS
AND I DON'T DO THAT
I DON'T LOSE MY HEAD
I DON'T TOSS MY HAT
I'VE TRIED IT ALL
AT LEAST ONCE BEFORE

BRIAN:
BUT I DON'T DO THAT
NO NO NO NO NO

DOUG:
I DON'T DO THAT
NO NO NO NO NO

BRIAN & DOUG:
WE DON'T DO THAT
ANYMORE
(Spoken) We don't do that.
(Sung) ANYMORE

(CHRISTOPHER enters as BRIAN and DOUG exit. He is wearing a flowing robe and has his hair wrapped in a towel – like a grand movie star of yore.)

CHRISTOPHER:
maybe i'd seen
too many t.v. movies
of the week
but i thought
terminal diseases
were inherently dramatic

oh mine was
at first
but when the worst
had passed
that fast trip
to the hospital
intensive care
and then recovering to where
i could go home
go back to work
and make it through
the day
well hey
it was just the same
old boring shit
like before

i wanted more
i wanted neat dramatic takes
building to commercial breaks
i wanted mother
to be played by liza
struggling to entertain me
through her tears
i wanted fireworks
i wanted draaaaaama
not dull routines
of a.z.t.
another test
one more i.v.
and all the rest
mundanity

oh why can't death
be like t.v.

(CHRISTOPHER takes a seat.)

(DWIGHT enters.)

DWIGHT:
i didn't know
what else to do
no auditions
coming through
hadn't worked
in far too long
the room i'd had
for just a song
was locked one day
when i came back
and all my stuff
stacked in the hall
i had to call the folks
and borrow money
to go home

funny
i should call it that
i felt
like i'd been born in hell
escaped
and lived to tell the tale
of growing up
the tainted son
of fundamentalists
from whom i'd run
the opposite direction

i had a voice
and made the choice
to sing secular creations
despite my parents' protestations

i knew the scores
of all the shows by heart
and got a start
in "up with people"[1]
pretty corny
but some of us were horny
for the big time
and auditioned
for a broadway tour

sure enough
i got it
that was my finest hour
why did such sweetness
turn so sour

[1] *Directors outside the U.S. may substitute "at disneyland".*

to get my folks
to take me in
i had to ask forgiveness
for my sin
when they saw the chance
to win a wayward soul to christ
they agreed to take me back
which turned out pleasant
as the rack

as i lay there
hurting so
i was surrounded
by fanatics
wailing, screaming

(ALL on stage wail and moan.)

DWIGHT: *(Continued)*
cheap dramatics
in unrecorded tongues
and i used the air
left in my lungs
to sing the scores
of all the shows i knew
to drown them out
but they would shout
"be gone, satan"

ALL ON STAGE: Be gone!

DWIGHT:
"take your demon music
back below"

ALL ON STAGE: Satan!

DWIGHT:
and i would crow,
"don't you see
that this is hell
what could possibly be worse
didn't jesus say
'love and nurse the sick
embrace those who transgress'
where is he
in this sorry mess"

perhaps christ heard
that anguished scream
for then i drifted
in a dream
of a lovely broadway show
where i was left
to sing so beautifully
that angels were applauding me

a miracle
that last reprieve
allowing me
to take my leave
lost in dreams
of make believe

(REBECCA enters as DWIGHT sits.)

REBECCA:
everyone said i was crazy
to marry him
"beneath your station"
or
"why a man from iowa
when kansas is full o' good ones"
or
"a family like that
marked by disease
must be payin' for sins
hidin' somewhere
in their family trees"

but i liked him
and his folks
and even though
he and all his brothers
had hemophilia
the experts assured us
it was carried
by the mothers
and therefore our sons
would not suffer that affliction

and they didn't
not our boys
darryl and little gus
but somethin' else was wrong
they weren't like other babies
but sickly and distressed

before too long
we found out it was aids
my husband got it
from treatments
for his useless blood
passed it on to me
and we gave it to the boys
gave them death
as surely as we gave them life

i watched my babies die
and then my gus
only me
was left of us
and then my mind
began to go

other people let me know
that i was actin' strange
like at the church dinner
when i opened up
the salt shaker
and dumped the contents all over
everyone's meal
then cried and cried
and screamed
and started takin' off my clothes
to let the demons out

i had one last reprieve
of sudden clarity
when i could see
what needed to be done

i took a gun
which gus had left
shot all the chickens
and the cats
then set fire
to the house and barn
went back
to get that special yarn
i ordered from des moines
and was eaten by the flames

they said i was crazy
wonder if i was
the lines are very hazy
'tween "why us"
and "because"

(CLAUDIA enters as REBECCA sits.)

CLAUDIA:
here's a little trick
to find out
who your friends really are
contract a terminal illness
then tell everyone you have it

make a list
cross off those
who insist on asking
"how did you get it"
and under the heading
of "friends who are true"
mark those who ask
"what can i do?"

my news caused such a flurry
of liberal concern
at the company
where i'd been pointed to with pride
as proof
executives in charge of sales
did not entirely consist
of caucasian males

oh the rallying round
of well-intentioned types
who really showed their stripes
by asking the wrong questions

anyone who did
was banished from the realm
and i was virtually alone
at the helm of my careering life
wondering what the hell i'd do
when the killer
coursing through my body
reached full concentration

then my secretary

(ANGELA enters.)

CLAUDIA: *(Continued)*
something of a sight
in outfits more appropriate for night
closed the office door
burst into tears
and then apologies

having worked for me for years
she knew my moods
and needs
and even fears
instinctively
and made my life of dying
much easier for me

(CLAUDIA and ANGELA sit together.)

she was there
and showed her genuine concern
and care
by reading to me
when i became too ill
to do so on my own

i requested proust and woolf
and gertrude stein
she tried
but could not get through
two sentences of those
as an alternative
she chose
books she'd read her children

i soon knew every fairy tale
and kiddie ditty by heart
and then she'd start again
and i would sigh
"go back
you have a life
and your family needs feeding"
but she would just continue reading

she only stopped
when i did too
the company threw
a tasteful little service
which she was not invited to

they treated her
my one true friend
worse than they did me
but she will have my gratitude
for all eternity

(Music in.)

(ANGELA sings to CLAUDIA.)

'I DON'T KNOW HOW TO HELP YOU"

ANGELA:
ALL THE FAIRY TALES HAVE HAPPY ENDINGS
EVEN THOUGH THE PASSAGE CAN BE ROUGH
WE'VE BEEN IN THE FOREST FOR A LONG TIME
SO WHEN WILL ALL OUR TRIALS BE ENOUGH
NOW YOU HAVE BEEN WOUNDED BY THE DRAGON
AND PROVED YOURSELF A HERO ALL ALONG
I WISH THAT I COULD HEAL YOU
WITH THE LOVE I FEEL
OR FIND THE POTION THAT WOULD MAKE YOU
    STRONG

I DON'T KNOW HOW TO HELP YOU
I DON'T KNOW WHAT TO SAY
I WISH THAT I COULD WAVE A WAND
AND CHASE THE HURT AWAY
THAT WOULD TAKE MORE MAGIC
THAN MAKING GOLD FROM HAY
AND THOUGH I'M ONLY HUMAN
I AM HERE TO STAY

WISH THERE WAS A BOOK WITH ALL THE ANSWERS
OR ARTICLES THAT SPELLED OUT WHAT TO DO
I WOULD TRACK DOWN EXPERTS OR OPINIONS
IF THEY'D TELL ME HOW I COULD HELP YOU
BUT NO ONE SEEMS TO KNOW OF A SOLUTION
OR EVEN IF THERE WILL BE ONE SOME DAY
I WISH THAT I COULD FIND YOU
SOME SMALL PEACE OF MIND
OR PROMISE THERE'S AN ANSWER ON THE WAY

BUT I DON'T KNOW HOW TO HELP YOU
I DON'T KNOW WHAT TO SAY
I WISH THAT I COULD WAVE A WAND
AND CHASE THE HURT AWAY
BUT THAT WOULD TAKE MORE MAGIC
THAN MAKING GOLD FROM HAY
AND THOUGH I'M ONLY HUMAN
I AM HERE TO STAY
I AM HERE
ALWAYS HERE
I AM HERE TO STAY

*(ROSCOE enters grandly from far Upstage wearing a black
     ballgown.)*

ROSCOE:
honey
i figured
since this was my swan song
i was going to play it
for all it was fucking worth

on one of my early visits
to one of my early doctors
i collapsed in the waiting room
and received the most delicious attention
that's when i realized
i could do this episode
like a true blue diva
and go out
in a blaze of style
not seen
since garbo
graced the silver screen

i took to wearing
lots of black
pearls cascading down my back
a tasteful camellia
behind one ear
sometimes a veil
it was *so* queer
but they'd remember
when i was gone
so i just carried on
and on

all my life
i'd been tormented
by the fearful
and demented creeps
who didn't see
that laughter keeps
the soul so free
even death
would smile at me

and in the end
there on that ward
i truly gained
my life's reward

an audience

(EVERYONE on stage jeers, cheers and applauds as ROSCOE
impersonates female film stars – Davis, Hepburn, Mae West,
etc. – during the following.)

ROSCOE: *(Continued)*
captive
and enthralled
the odd venue
where i was called
to entertain
the challenge
to erase the pain
for just awhile
to get a laugh
or cause a smile
where none had been
for many days
show biz works
in wondrous ways

so now you know
this diva's story
ended in
a blaze of glory

(ROSCOE freezes in a grand pose as HELEN enters nearby.)

HELEN:
i didn't want a soul to know

if word got out
that i had that
fear would flood
the laundromat
who would want
to wash her clothes
in machines
which had held those
of someone
now touched by a plague

what would people think
i knew they would create a stink
or nod and wink
behind my back
the ones too frightened to attack

my daughter meg
the firebrand
would have sued
the doctors
who never came
to the conclusion
that the source
was a transfusion

but i said no
i did not cotton to attention
did not relish
mention of my name
in connection with this shame
still don't like it
when heads tilt
to read my name
here on this quilt

i made no fuss
and did my dying on a ward
the only place i could afford
filled with types
i never dreamed of

(SHE acknowledges ROSCOE warily.)

wasn't that
fate's final kicker
freaks and grandma
getting sicker

before i knew it
i was caring
despite whatever
they were wearing
and they enjoyed my company
who'd have thought it
mercy me

it's good to make friends
as you go
but better other folks
don't know

(ROSCOE offers HELEN his hand and THEY cross and sit together.)

(WALTER enters.)

WALTER:
home
was such sweet medicine
the mountain breezes
cooled my fear
the untouched vistas
left me feeling near
the undeniable intelligence
which created the myriad details
of natural beauty
the wild jazz
of a hundred birds
a shock of sunflowers
underlining the purple mountains
the pure crisp air
filling my tired lungs
with hope

dad said
"well, son,
if you're sick
you'd better come on home"

not many secrets
in that town
word got out
that i was back
before i girded for attack

i got a call
anonymous
which said
"wish you were dead"
and "don't come
to the school reunion"

i was numb with fright
when i limped into the room
that night
i had always been
the different one
cruel youth had its fun
at my expense
jokes had been my sole defense

then april
still as tall and lean
as when she was homecoming queen
said "walter
walter is that you"
came floating through
the crowd and said
loud enough for all to hear
"our walter has come home"

those words were like
the first few drops of rain
which led to showers
of kindness
from that community

there is no immunity
to fear
but those dear people
conquered that disease
with care
and my old pop
harvested a crop
of decency
in that time
of our despair

somewhere
there is an undeniable intelligence
behind the beauty
of that place
and in the love
on that town's face

(Music in as WALTER sits. ANGELA and JUDITH enter, observing him.)

"CELEBRATE"

ANGELA:
IF WE CAN LEARN ANY LESSON
FROM THESE ACRES OF GRIEF
IT'S TO LIVE FOR WHAT WE HAVE NOW

JUDITH:
IF THERE'S A PATH TO COMFORT
OR A ROAD TO RELIEF
I KNOW YOU'LL TAKE ME THERE SOMEHOW

ANGELA & JUDITH:
FINDING THIS FRIENDSHIP
HAS RESTORED MY BELIEF
IN THE JOY THAT FATE WILL ALLOW
SO LET'S GRAB THE MOMENT
NO REASON TO WAIT
LET'S TAKE A MOMENT
TO CELEBRATE

ANGELA:
CELEBRATE

JUDITH:
CELEBRATE THAT WINTER TURNS TO SPRING
CELEBRATE

ANGELA:
CELEBRATE THE LIFE THE RAIN WILL BRING

ANGELA & JUDITH:
APPRECIATE THE SEASONS THAT WE SHARE
CELEBRATE EACH MOMENT
'CAUSE EACH ONE WITH YOU IS RARE

ANGELA:
WE HAVE WEATHERED THE STORM
WE HAVE MET THE TEST

JUDITH:
WE HAVE SEEN THE WORST
WE HAVE KNOWN THE BEST

ANGELA & JUDITH:
FOUND GREAT FRIENDS TO SHARE THE WEIGHT
LET'S TAKE THIS MOMENT TO CELEBRATE

JUDITH:
CELEBRATE

ANGELA:
CELEBRATE THAT MORNING FOLLOWS NIGHT
CELEBRATE

JUDITH:
CELEBRATE THAT WOUNDED BIRDS TAKE FLIGHT

JUDITH & ANGELA:
COMMEMORATE THE LOVE OF THOSE WHO'VE GONE
CELEBRATE THIS MOMENT
AND THAT LIFE IS GOING ON

ANGELA & JUDITH:
CELEBRATE
CELEBRATE THAT WINTER TURNS TO SPRING
CELEBRATE
CELEBRATE THE LIFE THE RAIN WILL BRING

ANGELA:
APPRECIATE

JUDITH:
APPRECIATE

ANGELA & JUDITH:
THE SEASONS THAT WE SHARE

JUDITH:
CELEBRATE WITH MUSIC

ANGELA:
CELEBRATE WITH LAUGHTER

ANGELA & JUDITH:
CELEBRATE EACH MOMENT

ANGELA:
FEELS SO GOOD TO CELEBRATE

ANGELA & JUDITH:
CELEBRATE
CELEBRATE
CELEBRATE!

(LAMAR ambles on.)

LAMAR:
first time i'm in hospital
lady axes
my social security number

"ain't got one
don't do me no good
on the street"

social-worker lady
she look beat
and say

(A wicked imitation)

"you should call
these people"
and i do
'cause it seem
that there might be
a buck or two
somewhere for me

so this white boy
blushin' honky red
come by and said
he do the paper work
and sure enough
i get some bread

but then
he keep on comin' back
even when i'm out
and lyin' round my crib

he rub his nose
all time
like smell o' my room
bother him or sumpin'
and he get upset
when i score some shit
to make me happy

he play
honky judge and jury
and flush that stuff
in one big hurry

when i get bad
he take me
to 'mergency at bellevue
crazies in cuffs
kids bleedin' and stuffs
and i wants a smoke
he say,

(Another outrageous impersonation.)

"you can't smoke here"
and i say,
"you such a white boy
wheel me behind that curtain"
so he do
and i gets my smoke

one time i say,
"sonny
i'm gonna steal money
from the nurse's purses
'cause i am hep
to where they kept"
and he get pissed off
and say
"you do that
and those nurses
will fuck you over
like you never been
fucked over before"
a door open
in my head
i sit up in bed
"hey, you a faggot?"
he look hard at me and say,
"some people call us that"
he too much
"some people call us that"

but he all right
the sight o' him
at my funeral
in the bronx
make me laugh
only white boy
and everybody scream
and carry on

but hey
that faggot
blushin' honky red
keep comin' back
even when i'm dead

(Shaking his head, LAMAR takes his seat.)

(RAFAELA enters.)

RAFAELA:
i was a big girl
i knew the score
messed around
went back for more
played the game
with mr. jones
never shared his habits
but they crept into my bones

but hey
like i say
i was a big girl
and big girls don't cry
they take their mistakes
and die
without jumping
into lakes of tears
they say
"fuck you world
i've had enough
unless you're into
playing rough
don't mess with me
'cause i'm a big girl"

but not my child
my sweet arlette
not old enough
to think of boyfriends yet
but wise enough to know
that others in the barrio
would burn us out
if they discovered
what my sickness was about

so my sweet girl
not even ten
became the woman of the house
and i became her child
totally dependent
on her make-shift meals
her daring deals
to get prescriptions
her descriptions
of the world beyond
my bed

i don't ask for pity
don't cry because i'm dead
but somewhere in the city
is an angel
a tiny gem
a pearl
who learned exactly
what it means
to be a big
big girl

(RAFAELA takes her seat.)

(NANCY enters.)

NANCY:
at first
none of our nurses
wanted anything to do
with anyone
with aids

that made me crazy
'cause i was gay
and therefore safe
at least at first
but not from seeing
old friends die

so i volunteered
for the new aids ward
and in about two minutes flat
i realized that
professional standards
did not apply
i just had to cry
and help these people die

they needed hugs
and common decency
much more
than some invasive test
which might prolong their lives
for twenty minutes more
at best

i stood it
for a couple years
until my well
ran dry of tears

the day before
my leave was due
a pregnant woman
crazed on crack
had to be restrained
while i was giving
an injection
her hand got loose
i pricked myself
with her infection

i found my way
back to my ward
by quite a different road
but now
many like me
helped with the load
of details and of boredom
that dying holds in store
and i was very proud to be
back in that place once more

sometimes we make a difference
by doing what we must
and leave some small impression
in life's enduring dust

(NANCY remains in place as KHADIJA enters.)

    KHADIJA:
i was always sick
and nobody would pick
a baby who had aids
to make their very own
so the hospital was home

my mommy went away
and there was no one else to say
that i belonged to them

but nearly every day
someone came to play
doctors or nurses
ladies with big purses
that usually held some presents
and even caretakers
were always checking in on me
which is like a family
is s'posed to be

sometimes i'd see
kids with parents
on t.v.
and wonder
what is wrong with me

(Music in. NANCY offers KHADIJA her hand and THEY take their
*   seats as the SINGERS enter.)*

"HEROES ALL AROUND"

DOUG:
IN THE CANYONS OF DEATH
FRIENDS LIE IN A DAZE
SILENTLY FIGHTING
THEIR WAY THROUGH THE HAZE
MANY UNCONSCIOUS
TO ALL SIGHT AND SOUND
THOUGH THEY LIE THERE UNMOVING
THEY ARE HEROES ALL AROUND

BRIAN:
IN APARTMENTS AND WARDS
THE ANGELS DESCEND
TO COOL A FEVER
TO SIT WITH A FRIEND
TO FILL IN THE VOID
WHERE NO FAMILY IS FOUND
THOUGH THEY'D NEVER ADMIT IT
THEY ARE HEROES ALL AROUND

JUDITH & ANGELA:
THEY ARE OUT THERE RIGHT NOW
FIGHTING A WAR
CREATING MIRACLES
WORKING FOR MORE
THEIR DEEDS UNREWARDED
THEIR GLORY UNCROWNED
NO MISSIONS RECORDED
BUT THERE ARE HEROES ALL AROUND

ALL SINGERS:
WE ALL CAN BE HEROES
BY GIVING A HAND
RUNNING AN ERRAND
OR MAKING A STAND
LET'S FIGHT HEAVEN'S SORROW
WITH FEET ON THE GROUND
IN THE WAR FOR TOMORROW
WE NEED HEROES ALL AROUND
WE NEED HEROES
WE NEED HEROES
WE NEED HEROES

*(The musical figure continues as the SINGERS exit and PAUL
     enters Upstage, standing at attention.)*

PAUL:
i couldn't wait
to go to viet nam[1]

(Music out.)

PAUL: *(Continued)*
i loved my country
though the pansies
and the preppies
said we fought
for no good reason
i called it treason
to doubt our elected leaders
those pinkos
and liberal-hearted bleeders
had no idea
what goes on
in the real world

---

[1] *Pronounced to rhyme with "Sam".*

i was young
too green to understand
what i'd gotten into
but it was easy to get out
powders and potions
laying all about
so cheap and easy
sliding into dreams
so quick
the silencing of screams
heard earlier that day
screams of boys
no longer here to play
in fields of poppies
and of spice

(HE pantomimes taking a big snort of some substance.)

nice

and eventually euphoria
"you're going home"
yo!
let's go!

i loved my country
took an oath
no more needles
no more dope
now my veins
were full of hope

parades are nice
jobs are better
we had neither
got a letter
from my fiancée
"hey sorry
what to say
met this guy
you were away"
so i searched out
my old friend from 'nam
course uncle sam
had raised the price
by quite a bit
and stepped on it
until it took a lot more shit
to hear the band
to fill my veins
with disneyland

i drifted
and one day awoke
to yet another cosmic joke
another war
a battle of the blood
the fuel of my dreams
attacked by some new enemy
and it advanced invisibly
through hypodermic legacy
until at last
it had found me

i was certain
somebody would do something
that in this country
i still loved somehow
and went to battle for
were soldiers who would fight for me

but silence
bullshit
nothing

*(PAUL addresses the ACTORS sitting behind him. THEY start
responding to the rest of his speech as though THEY are at a
protest rally.)*

PAUL: *(Continued)*
so many more
than died in 'nam
not killed by gooks
who gave a damn
but by neglect
of bureaucrats
we certainly did not elect
who ignored both threat and fact
and casually refused to act

ACTORS: Act Up! Act Up!

PAUL:
shame

ACTORS: Shame! Shame! Shame! Shame! Shame!

PAUL:
for shame
history will place the blame
on presidents
and pussy-footed troops
while our mothers
sit on stoops
and cry for those
lost needlessly

america
america
god shed
his shame
on thee

(PAUL turns and faces the part of the COMPANY so far assembled on the stage. HE raises his fist and yells:)

PAUL:
History will recall ...

ALL:
Bureaucrats did nothing at all!
History will recall
Bureaucrats did nothing at all!

PAUL:
Gay, Straight, Black, White!

ALL:
Same struggle, same fight!
Gay, Straight, Black, White!
Same struggle, same fight!

PAUL:
Act up! Fight back! Fight AIDS!

ALL:
Act up! Fight back! Fight AIDS!
We are everywhere! We are everywhere!
WE ARE EVERYWHERE!

(The CAST has been marching in place and is now facing Upstage, frozen with fists in the air. NAT, a minister or priest who has entered during the protest, surveys the scene with disgust.)

NAT:
go back
go back to your closets
can't you see
how unseemly you appear
shouting you are queer
well my dear
we did things differently
in my time
this aberration
was better left a crime

of course
god punished us
with sickness and disease
we would not please him
we would not be
what nature had intended
fitting
we were ended
in this unseemly manner

ALL:
We are everywhere! We are everywhere!
WE ARE EVERYWHERE!

(During the above lines the COMPANY faces front and sits.)

NAT:
especially those
who waved the banner
advertising our transgressions
to the world
my flag was not unfurled

i suffered for my sin
kept it well within the bounds
of moral approbation
and died in silent conflagration

blessed is the one who blames
his own creation of hell flames

(NAT takes a seat.)

(JOANNE enters solemnly, as if SHE is delivering bad news.)

    JOANNE:
if you should get
the diagnosis
and find your t-cell count
is dropping
i would offer this prognosis
time to do

(Shouting with glee.)

some heavy shopping

go ahead
and buy like mad
everything
you wish you had
take your plastic
and go crazy
final sprees
aren't for the lazy

don't stop to question
what you need
the point here
is to spend with speed
jaguars, jewelry
don't think twice
time shares
are especially nice

and may i offer
one last word
advice i wish
that i had heard
if spending
makes you feel alive
die before the bills arrive

(Music in as SINGERS enter.)

"SPEND IT WHILE YOU CAN"

(During the song, the SINGERS shower JOANNE with luxurious goods – jewels, furs, evening wear, a tiara.)

ANGELA:
CERTAIN FOLKS STACK UP THEIR GOLD
TUCK IT SAFELY IN THE HOLD
THEY FEAR THE FUTURE COULD BE ROUGH
AND DENY THEMSELVES A LOT OF STUFF

JOANNE: Not me!

ANGELA:
OTHER FOLKS ALLAY THEIR FRIGHT
PURCHASE EVERYTHING IN SIGHT
SNATCH UP TREATS TO THE LAST BON-BON
YOU CAN'T SPEND IT WHEN YOU'RE GONE

JOANNE: Oh, that's so true.

ALL SINGERS:
SPEND IT WHILE YOU CAN

JOANNE: Okay!

ALL SINGERS:
'CAUSE ONCE THE SHIT HAS HIT THE FAN
OR THE FAT IS IN THE FRYING PAN
YOU CAN'T BUY OFF THE REAPER MAN
YOU'D BETTER SPEND IT WHILE YOU CAN

ANGELA:	**JUDITH, DOUG, BRIAN:**
WHY LEAVE A PILE	OOOO, OOOO
FOR KIN YOU HATE?	KIN THAT YOU HATE
WHY LET THEM FIGHT	MONEY, MONEY
FOR YOUR ESTATE?	MONEY, MONEY
WHY LEAVE A CHUNK	
FOR THE GOVERNMENT MAN?	GOVERNMENT MAN

ALL SINGERS:
WHY NOT SPEND IT WHILE YOU CAN?
SPEND IT!

SPEND IT WHILE YOU CAN
'CAUSE ONCE THE SHIT HAS HIT THE FAN
OR THE FAT IS IN THE FRYING PAN
YOU CAN'T BUY OFF THE REAPER MAN
IF TREASURE FILLS YOUR CARAVAN
YOU'D BETTER SPEND IT
SPEND IT
SPEND IT
WHILE YOU CAN

(SINGERS exit.)

(BERTHA enters.)

BERTHA:
you know what gets my goat

legionnaire's disease
remember that one
please
few guys kick off
and you'd have thought
the world was ending

the powers
started sending
troops of eggheads
to investigate
and the great and mighty press
covered that inflated mess
like the second coming
or the first-time going

i saw the winds
of panic blowing
through that philadelphia hotel
i was working
where those veterans fell
and i was interviewed
and grilled
'til i felt
my brains had spilled
out of my head

i remembered all that fuss
when my man got aids
no one questioned us
no one seemed to care
no one said i should beware
of what he could pass on

course my man wasn't white
and never won a medal
for his fight
against the stuff
a battle which he lost
lord he paid a fearful cost

they don't have clubs for losers
no parades and no salutes
no conventions filled with boozers
spilling out of their old suits

not everyone's a legionnaire
my husband missed that boat
when i think back on their disease
i tell you
it gets my goat

(BERTHA takes her seat.)

(BUD enters.)

BUD:
weren't we a pretty pair
you bedridden
and incontinent
me covered with lesions
trying to take care of you
at home

our families
wonderful
my sister judith
the hot-shot lawyer
from the east
drew up our wills
airtight
so that our dying wish
could never be denied
and we would spend
eternity
sleeping side by side

and at your bed
your parents said
"you are an angel
to our son
the two of you
behave as one
our family plot
has room for you
when it is time
you'll be there too"

they stood beside me
at your grave
trying to be brave
as you were lowered
in the ground
what a lonely shocking sound

then your parents
turned around
and said
"you are a disgrace
we never want to see
your face again"

and the stress
of knowing
that the earth
would not caress us
there together
put me well under the weather

(JUDITH enters. She is his sister, the lawyer.)

BUD: *(Continued)*
my sister
took a leave of absence
nursed me to my end
then took an even longer stay
to remain here by the bay
and fight in court
she would not leave
until she could retrieve
your body

at last
we lie together
and leave behind
this legacy

surely
there is no dichotomy
as good
and bad
as family

(HE looks wistfully at JUDITH and crosses to her. THEY kiss.
    Music in as BUD sits.)

"MY BROTHER LIVED IN SAN FRANCISCO"

JUDITH:
MY BROTHER LIVED IN SAN FRANCISCO
HE SAID HE FINALLY FOUND HIS PLACE
AND WHEN I GO TO SAN FRANCISCO
EVERYWHERE I LOOK
I SEE HIS FACE

BUD AND I
FACED CHILDHOOD
UNDER STARK MONTANA SKIES
AND BUD
HE SEEMED TO ALWAYS HAVE
CITIES IN HIS EYES
HE LONGED FOR POSSIBILITY
HE LIVED TO MOVE AWAY
AND HE FINALLY FOUND HIS DREAM
IN THE CITY BY THE BAY

(JOE enters Upstage and is dimly lit.)

   JUDITH: *(Continued)*
JOE AND I
WERE BEST OF FRIENDS
IN OUR SMALL-TIME COLLEGE TOWN
AND JOE
HAD PERSONALITY
WHAT A CAMPUS CLOWN
HIS JOKES HID DEEPER RIVERS
WHICH BUBBLED FAR BELOW
AND HE RODE THE CURRENT WEST
WHERE THE RAPID WATERS FLOW

LOTS OF US
HAD BROTHERS THERE
WHO WOULD LOVE TO SHOW THE SIGHTS
AND SHARE
THE BALMY FREEDOM
OF SAN FRANCISCO NIGHTS
THEY LIKED IT SO MUCH MORE
THAN ANYWHERE THEY'D BEEN
AND WE THOUGHT THEY WOULD BE THERE
WHEN WE MADE IT BACK AGAIN

MY BROTHER LIVED IN SAN FRANCISCO
HE SAID HE FINALLY FOUND HIS PLACE
AND WHEN I GO TO SAN FRANCISCO
EVERYWHERE I LOOK
I SEE HIS FACE

(JUDITH exits.)

(JOE steps forward.)

    JOE:
after viewing the quilt
i told everyone
"if i die from aids
i want my panel
to be fabulous"

i was very clear
about this
i mentioned it
several times

so why
did i get
a beach towel
with hand-drawn lettering
and a teddy bear

a teddy bear
do you know
how many goddamn teddy bears
are on this quilt

i'm sorry
it's just not me

i deserve
something more
original
something special

like rock hudson
now there's a panel
that rainbow
those colors
the glitter

i know
i should not be bitter
at least
i was remembered

but i requested
fabulous

it isn't fair
to die
and then be
suffering from panel envy

(JOE takes his seat.)

(GRACE enters, and in the darkness, so does MILES.)

GRACE:
when the doctor told me
the meaning
of the purple spot
i started reading
everything

that was my way
to learn
all i could
and try to understand

where did this come from?
african monkeys
or experiments
gone astray
in secret labs
of c.i.a. apparatchiks
or was it
an unintended
side effect
of radiation
chemicals
or some other alteration
of the world of nature

and since the consequence
would surely be
the end
of what was known
as me
i read
all that had been said
of death
and found
a common thread
besides the tunnel
and the light
a sense
overwhelming and immense
of complete
and instant understanding

yes, i thought
that is it
that would be grace
to fully comprehend
why so many are suffering
why so many are dead or dying
why there are friends
and parents crying
why me

and if i understood
the tragedy of unearned death
perhaps i'd also understand
the mystery of lonely life
the need
the void
the endless tomes
the libraries
where longing roams

as i breathed
my rasping last
alone
i stopped the quest
for comprehending more
and let my self
so dark and sore
be filled with light
and peace
primary and expanding
a peace that passed
all understanding

*(As GRACE takes her seat, PATRICK rises from his and addresses
the audience.)*

PATRICK: *(Part II)*
i've told you
of the party
when i died
the celebration
of my life
which ended

but living is what mattered
and i lived
lived with aids
for years
fought the virus
indifference
and outright cruelty
surrounding it
fought each invader
of my body
fought my fear
of death
and the unknown

the fight sustained
and connected me
with others
who were fighting too
made life as rich
as it had ever been

you who hear me now
and also fight
you who know
the terror of the night
also know
that you are living with
not dying from
and that thin line
between your world
and mine
is an illusion
for on either side
of that divide
the truth is
we are going on

my friends
time will have its way
and all of must leave
but not before
one final tale
one story more
of lessons difficult to know
not giving up
but letting go

(PATRICK returns to his seat.)

(Light reveals MILES, already in place.)

   MILES:
i fought the end
with all my strength
determined to extend
the length
of this my time

i struggled so
to catch each breath
i would not be caught
by death

*(HE indicates DOUG, who has entered quickly, obviously
     concerned.)*

douglas
sitting there
in that awful
metal chair
where he had been
for months it seemed
was it that long
or had i dreamed
it all
this pallid room
the antiseptic based perfume
no
he had been there
all along
knowing love
would make me strong

(DOUG crosses in back of MILES and puts his arms around him.)

MILES: *(Continued)*
but finally
he held me
close
and tight
for seeming hours
in the night
and whispered
"let it go
you are fabulous
you know
have done
and given all you could
and none of us
would blame you
if you called it quits"

(DOUG releases MILES and crosses away.)

MILES: *(Continued)*
this is what
true love permits
the strength to say good-bye
when you are tired
too tired to try

it was not hard
to slip away
douglas holding me
that way
i think i smiled
at least inside
knowing love
had never died

(Music in as MILES bows his head. DOUG sings.)

"LEARNING TO LET GO"

DOUG:
MY NEPHEW SCOTT
IS READY TO START WALKING
HE GRABS MY LEG TO REACH A NEW PLATEAU
SOON HE'LL BE EXPLORING NEW DIRECTIONS
ALL IT TAKES IS LEARNING TO LET GO

MY SISTER JANE
HAS BEEN SO UNDERSTANDING
THERE'S NO NEED TO EXPLAIN, SHE SEEMS TO KNOW
SHE HOLDS SCOTT WITH SUCH LOVE AND PROTECTION
BUT SOME DAY SHE'LL BE LEARNING TO LET GO

(MILES stands and slowly crosses to join the rest of the COMPANY as DOUG sings to him.)

DOUG: *(Continued)*
THANK YOU
FOR BEING MY FOUNDATION
FOR GIVING ME A BOOST
WHEN I WAS LOW
YOUR COURAGE
IS MY INSPIRATION
GUESS IT'S TIME
I'M LEARNING TO LET GO

I'M THANKFUL YOU
COULD GET TO KNOW MY FAM'LY
AND WISH THAT YOU WERE HERE TO SEE SCOTT GROW
HE'S HOLDING ON LIKE THERE IS NO TOMORROW
AND ALL OF US ARE LEARNING TO LET GO

(To audience.)

I WANNA THANK YOU
FOR BEING MY FOUNDATION
FOR GIVING ME A BOOST
WHEN I WAS LOW
YOUR COURAGE
IS MY INSPIRATION
GUESS IT'S TIME
I'M LEARNING TO LET GO

*(The other SINGERS enter on one side of the stage and DOUG
    crosses to join them.)*

SINGERS:
THANK YOU
FOR BEING MY FOUNDATION
FOR GIVING ME A BOOST
WHEN I WAS LOW
YOUR COURAGE
IS MY INSPIRATION
GUESS IT'S TIME

I'M LEARNING TO LET GO
(As the SINGERS continue to repeat the chorus, the ACTORS rise from their sitting positions, and ONE by ONE cross Downstage and throw confetti. Then THEY return to their place and join in singing the song.)

ALL:
THANK YOU
FOR BEING MY FOUNDATION
FOR GIVING ME A BOOST
WHEN I WAS LOW
YOUR COURAGE
IS MY INSPIRATION
GUESS IT'S TIME
I'M LEARNING TO LET GO

(At the end of the song, the CAST watches as DOUG throws confetti on the last note of music.)

DOUG:
GUESS IT'S TIME
I'M LEARNING TO LET GO

NOTES ON SET AND COSTUMES

Basic bleachers have proven very effective as a setting. Cast members who appear early can move around on them and then take a seat (at the end of "And the Rain Keeps Falling Down" for everyone up to that point and one-by-one thereafter) – until the bleachers are filled with the characters we've met. *Elegies ...* has also been staged using chairs for each actor, bringing to mind the third act of *Our Town* – certainly an appropriate allusion. The piece has been performed everywhere from small discos to grand theaters, but whatever the situation – simple is best.

The Names Project Quilt was a primary inspiration for *Elegies ...* and can be effectively utilized as part of a production, either actual panels or simulations of them. Local, national and international chapters of the Names Project have been most generous in lending quilt panels to various productions (call 415-882-5500 for information). A word of caution, however. The panels are so intense in terms of color and pattern that using them as a backdrop for the actors has proven to distract from both the power of the quilt and the effectiveness of the performances. I think the panels are more usefully displayed in the house, lobby or as a proscenium frame where they can supply an important context and be more fully appreciated for their own incredible power.

Orchestra placement depends very much on the space. Raised Upstage behind a scrim is great, center stage with bleachers on either side is fine, to one side of the stage or the other or below the stage on the auditorium floor have all proven workable.

Because *Elegies ...* is comprised of many individual units I've found it helpful to costume the cast in a single color (black or white have proven effective) to help unify the disperate pieces. Perhaps the singers could be costumed slightly differently (dressed in black and white?) to distinguish them from the rest.

With a cast of 36, the performers' bodies are the most effective (and economical) design element at your disposal. Starting with an empty stage and accumulating cast members one-by-one until the space is filled with people provides a powerful visual statement of AIDS' inexorable advance and ultimate toll.

MUSICALS

THE RED SNEAKS (**Little Theatre.**) Elizabeth Swados. 4m., 4f. Unit set. This free-wheeling contemporary musical for teens is an adaptation of the classic story "The Red Shoes," transposed to today's urban jungle. A loose adaptation. Ms. Swados has put together an allegorical montage of songs, scenes and monologues about a welfare hotel resident named Dedre who is persuaded by Shawn, a mysterious young drifter, to accept a pair of glittery red sneakers. Whoever is wearing them may wish for anything—and every wish comes true! Dedre, desperate for any means to escape her plight, takes the easy way out—the red sneaks—which puts her on a fast trip to an early death. "The most refreshing thing about *The Red Sneaks* ... is the chance to hear youths rather than adults talk about the nightmarish pressures of urban life."—N.Y. Times "Remarkably clear, unsentimental and disturbing ...a gritty little musical that combines pop and rock with more traditional musical comedy."—A.P. "A most effective contemporary morality play ... the music has real gusto."—N.Y. Post.   (#20902)

MIDSUMMER NIGHTS (**All Groups.**) Book & Lyrics by Brian D. Leys. Music by Kevin Kuhn. 6m., 8f. Unit set. Imagine Shakespeare's *A Midsummer Night's Dream* crossed with *Grease* and *Beach Blanket Bingo*, and you will only begin to get the idea of this whacky new show. The musical is narrated by Puck, a charming beach-bum who is backed up by a girl-group chorus of three girls in early sixties bikinis (tame, by today's standards) whose names are—you guessed it—Moth, Peaseblossom and Cobweb. Shakespeare's young lovers are now typical high school kids of the period. One's an archetypal nerd, another an air-headed beach boy. Theseus is now the high school gym coach. Oberon and Titania have been re-cast as delightfully out of place refugees from the previous decade—they are a pair of beatniks ("Cool, Daddy-o"). Bottom is now Fred Bottom. He runs the local Dodge dealership and is a ham-actor in the local community theatre. His daughter, the local fast girl, has the hots for the nerdy son of the Hippolyta character—who is now the matronly English teacher. Amazingly, Shakespeare's basic plot fits right into American culture as celebrated by the Beach Boys and Jan & Dean—and, let us not forget, the immortal Annette Funicello and Frankie Avalon. You'll have quite a beach party with this delightful show, and we predict your audiences will wanna get up and twist and shout with you! "It is a frothy show with lively tunes and some sassy and clever lyrics."—N.Y. Times. "A charming endeavor. Lively and cute. A great deal of fun."—Newark Star-Ledger. Needless to say this terrific new show is perfect for high school and college production.   (#14953)

FAVORITE MUSICALS *from*

"The House of Plays"

A FINE AND PRIVATE PLACE

(All Groups) Book & Lyrics by Erik Haagensen. Music by Richard Isen. Adapted from the novel by Peter S. Beagle. 3m., 2f, (may be played by 2m., 2f.) + 1 raven (may be either m. or f.) Ext. setting. "The grave's a fine and private place,/But none, I think, do there embrace." Little did you know, Andrew Marvell, that someday, someone would come up with a charming love story, set in a graveyard, about two lost souls who are buried there, who meet and fall in love. Also inhabiting the cemetery is an eccentric old man who has the gift of being able to see and converse with the inhabitants of the graves, as well as with a raven who swoops in at mealtimes with some dinner he has swiped for the old guy. Also present from time to time is a delightful old Jewish widow, whose husband Morris is buried in the cemetery. She often stops by to tell Morris what's new. Her name is Gertrude, and it is soon apparent that she also stops by to flirt with old Jonathan Rebeck (she doesn't know he actually *lives* there). A crisis arises when it appears the young couple will be separated. The young man, it seems, has been deemed a suicide and, as such, he must be removed from consecrated ground. Their only hope is Jonathan; but to help them Jonathan must come out in the open. Had we but world enough, and time, we would tell you how Jonathan manages to salvage the romance; but we'll just have to hope the above story intrigues you enough to examine the delightful libretto and wonderfully tuneful music for yourself. A sell-out, smash hit at the Goodspeed in Connecticut and, later, at the American Stage Co. in New Jersey (the professional theatre which premiered *Other People's Money),* this happy, whimsical, sentimental, up-beat new show will delight audiences of all ages. . **(#8154)**

FAVORITE MUSICALS *from* "The House of Plays"

PHANTOM

(All Groups) Book by Arthur Kopit. Music & Lyrics by Maury Yeston. Large cast of m. & f. roles—doubling possible. Various Ints. & Exts. This sensational new version of Gaston Leroux' *The Phantom of the Opera* by the team which gave you *Nine* wowed audiences and critics alike with its beautiful music and lyrics, and expertly crafted book, which gives us more background information on beautiful Christine Daee and the mysterious Erik than even the original novel does. Christine is here an untrained street singer discovered by Count Philippe de Chandon, champagne tycoon. Erik, the Phantom of the Opera, is the illegitimate son of a dancer and the opera's manager. He becomes obsessed with the lovely Christine because her voice reminds him of his dead mother's. "Reminiscent of *The Hunchback of Notre Dame, Cyrano de Bergerac* and *The Elephant Man, Phantom*'s love story—and the passionately soaring music it prompts—are deliciously sentimental. Add Erik's father lovingly acknowledging his parenthood as his son is dying and the show jerks enough tears to fill that Paris Opera Lagoon."—San Diego Union. "Yeston and Kopit get us to care about the characters by telling us a lot about them, some of it funny, but most of it poignant."—Houston Chronicle. **(#18958)**